VOLTRON
LEGENDARY DEFENDER

Hunk's Story

By Cala Spinner

Illustrated by Patrick Spaziante

Ready-to-Read

Simon Spotlight
New York London Toronto Sydney New Delhi

SIMON SPOTLIGHT
An imprint of Simon & Schuster Children's Publishing Division
1230 Avenue of the Americas, New York, New York 10020
This Simon Spotlight edition December 2018
Manufactured in the United States of America 1118 LAK
2 4 6 8 10 9 7 5 3 1
ISBN 978-1-5344-3209-3 (hc)
ISBN 978-1-5344-3208-6 (pbk)
ISBN 978-1-5344-3210-9 (eBook)

Hi there. I'm Hunk.
I'm the Paladin of the Yellow Lion.
That means I'm one of five pilots
who come together to form a
big space robot called Voltron.
Also, I'm a leg . . .
the left leg, to be exact!

I didn't always want
to be a Paladin.
When I was little,
I wanted to be an engineer.

I always liked putting things
together and figuring out
how they work.
I never signed up to save anyone.

When I was accepted into a school called the Galaxy Garrison, I was so excited!

I was a good engineer,
but I got sick a lot because of
motion sickness.
Even though I tried my hardest,
I barfed in the main gearbox
during an important spaceship test.
My teacher, Commander Iverson,
was not happy.

One night, my friend Lance
decided to sneak out.
I wanted to stay back at
the Garrison.
I didn't want to get in trouble.

Lance convinced me to go out,
and it changed my whole life.
That night we met three students,
named Pidge, Shiro, and Keith.

Keith discovered a kind of energy.
He wasn't sure what it was.
I built a device to help us find out
where the energy was coming from.
It used energy patterns to show us
the way.

It was the first time I'd felt useful in a long time!

My device led us to the Blue Lion, one of five ships that form Voltron. We boarded the lion and took off.

Then we met two aliens,
named Princess Allura and Coran.
They explained that Voltron is a
robot that defends the universe.
Suddenly, I got the feeling
I'd have a cooler job,
and a scarier one, than being
a Garrison engineer.

Allura said that I would
pilot the Yellow Lion.
She said it has a mighty heart
and puts the needs of others first.
Allura thought we would be a
good match.

I didn't think I was anything like
the Yellow Lion.
All I wanted was to go home,
but then I met the Yellow Lion
and we bonded instantly.
I felt like throwing up a lot less!

Allura explained that Voltron needed to defeat evil aliens called the Galra. The Galra had destroyed her planet and forced many others into slavery.

I knew that Voltron was important. I didn't know how important it was until I visited a kind of living planet called a Balmera.

There, I met aliens named Rax
and Shay.
The Galra forced them to live
underground and work for them.
Seeing that made me realize
just how bad the Galra are.

Thanks to Voltron
and Allura's guidance,
we were able to free the Balmerans.
I had never felt prouder.

Of course, not all Voltron
missions have been so
successful.
During one mission,
the other Paladins and
I visited a space mall.

We were supposed to look for an object called a Scaultrite Lens, but I was hungry, and the food court looked interesting!

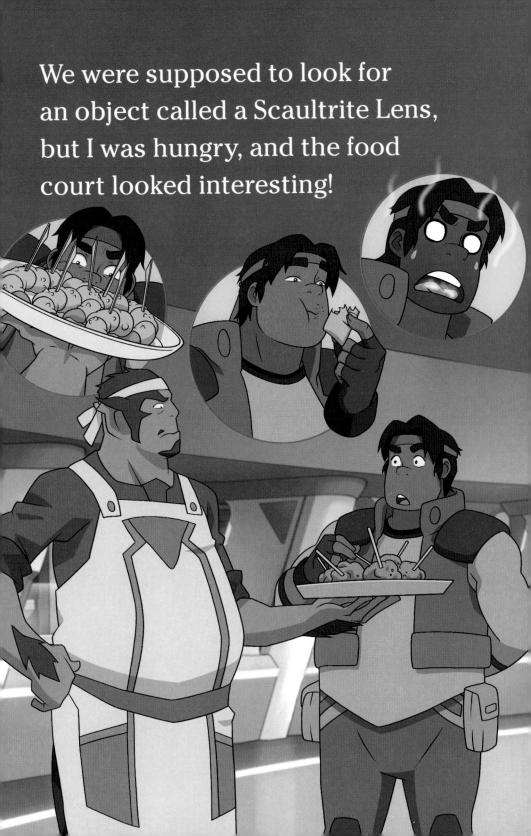

That is how I learned that in space, there is no such thing as "free." An alien named Vrepit Sal made me work in his kitchen. Although I was only supposed to wash dishes, I convinced him to make me head chef.

Of course, I couldn't stay for long.
I had a universe to save!
But working at Sal's made me
realize something else, too.

But as a cook,
I brought people together.
Through cooking,
I could make people happy!

As we started freeing other planets,
I brought leaders together by
making my most popular dish.
It is called pigs in blankets.

Maybe Allura was right after all.
Although I had wanted to go home,
I started putting the
needs of others first,
just like the Yellow Lion.

If I ever go back to Earth,
I'd like to have a word
with my old teacher,
Commander Iverson.

I'd tell him all about what
it means to be part of a team.
I'd say that it's okay for students
to get motion sickness.
They can still amount to something.

Then I'd show other future space explorers that happiness comes from serving others.

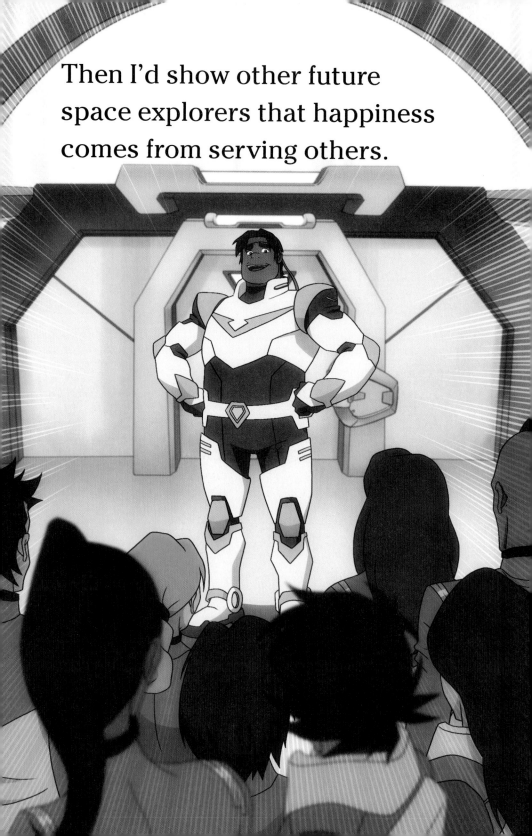

That's why one of my favorite things to do is to cook for the team!

I may not have wanted to be a
Paladin at first, but in the end,
it will all be worth it.
Besides, if I'm really lucky,
maybe I'll see Shay again!